leela

A *Play* of Appearance and Presence

A Novel By

Sankarasubramanyan Ramamoorthy

ISBN 979-888591297-6

Contents

Acknowledgements

Thanks to Wasundhara, Awantika, Kirti, Sharad, Renuka and Lalitha for reviewing my book and providing valuable suggestions. Thanks Wasundhara for editing and providing suggestions for cover design.

I dedicate this book to my three sisters - *Tangamani, Leela and Lalitha* and my brother – *Ramani.*

ब्रह्म सत्यं जगन्मथ्यिा जीवो ब्रह्मैव नापर: ।
Brahma-Satyam Jagan-Mithyā Jivo Brahmaiva Nāparaḥ
(Brahman is the truth, the world is an appearance and
the Self is that Brahman)
Sankaracharya

Prologue

We had a tall guava tree at home and as a child, my favorite pastime was to climb onto a branch high up on that tree. I would sit there for hours watching the road, the bus stop, people going by and the world of animals and plants around me. I would follow the squirrels as they scurried around branches and then suddenly become still as if listening to some melody and rushing off again. Sometimes I thought the Squirrel looked at me wondering "what is this Boy doing here on top of a tree?"

I saw the world change constantly in front of my eyes, every season, every day, and every moment. Nothing remained constant. I changed too. I grew up and stopped climbing that tree. One day, the tree was also brought down to make way for a construction.

This fascination for the world and its changing nature has remained with me all these years. I often wonder if it is just a play that nature puts up for all to see with the scenes changing all the time. Like the Bard said *"All the world's a stage, And all the men and women merely players…"*

A Leela (play) of appearances. In this play, I too am one of the characters, a special appearance!

Once I slept on that branch and fell. Luckily, it was just after the rains, and I fell on a lush green lawn. Except for some bruises, I was alright. My mother heard the story and said a prayer to her God. In my mind I was curious. Did that "God" save me? When I say "luck" was that a reference to the God? If nature and I are appearances, can my mother's God be any different?

My curiosity brings me to this book. Please join me in this journey as we explore the play of appearance of the world, me, and God. Maybe you will discover the presence beyond all that. The presence in which all appears, comes, and goes.

Sankar

February 1, 2022

Appearances without reality is impossible, for then, what could appear? Reality without appearance would be nothing, for there is nothing outside appearances"
F.H. Bradley (1893)

CHAPTER ONE

DREAMING

We are meeting at a roadside café decorated with scenes from Mardi Gras, probably from a long time ago. The small round tables in the café are covered with a white and red checkered tablecloth. The place is mostly empty except for three other tables occupied by what looks like students from the nearby university.

We sit at our usual table, and I decide to order coffee and ginger buscuits, while drooling over the pink and green macaroons by the display desk. Maya is opting for a green leaf herbal tea with nothing to eat.

We have been coming here for many years now. The café has changed ownership, changed its décor and so too some of the staff. However, for us it's the same café. Maybe the energy is the same and even the coffee. We treat some spaces in our lives based on our mental images created when we first went there. The space might change physically but our mental image of that space is somewhere deeply rooted in our mind's eye, and we refuse the see the changed space. This café is one such space for us. It is our space of comfort, familiarity, and memories. Maybe there are better cafes in town now, but we prefer to come here regardless.

Maybe when things change drastically, the mental image struggles to find familiarity from the past. I had that experience when I went to see my school in Cochin. The road was familiar, but the old school building was demolished and a new one has come in its place. I felt a deep sense of loss and felt like a stranger to a space where I was present for ten years of my life. I had a déjà vu experience when I found the large tree in the courtyard still standing majestically there. It was like a talisman that connected me to the spirit of the place. I wished trees can speak and I could tell the Tree I'm that Boy who studied and played here five decades ago.

My wandering mind was brought back to the present by the Waiter who came to collect our orders. There was a time when we were thoughtless and gorged macaroons and cakes with coffee. Now that I have put on a few inches and have a bald pate, biscuits seem a rational choice and I tell myself, "I'm saving calories for the fourth pint later tonight". So, I ordered my usual coffee and buscuits and Maya ordered her tea.

The other day I was at a hotel lobby, and someone said hello to me and introduced himself as a classmate of mine from my university days. I just couldn't place this person at all. I could feel my mind in overdrive trying to retrieve any traces of memory about this person, without success. He was puzzled that I showed no recognition and started asking me questions to verify whether his assumption of me was true. I answered his questions correctly and my identity was established within him. However, that was not the case with me. His appearance showed no resemblance to the millions of pictures of people stored in my memory. Thankfully his taxi arrived, and he said a quick "great meeting you" and rushed to the foyer. I heaved a sigh of relief, but I felt let down by my mind. I also fell two notches in my own estimation for my significant ability to recall information.

Like that Gentleman at the hotel lobby (whom I haven't identified still!) our appearances have also changed significantly over the last twenty years. When we met, me and Maya looked much younger, more energetic, adventurous…it seems like we have become less of ourselves as we age. While we have changed physically, energetically, and mentally I believe we are still the same person. My appearance to the world has changed, though Mom treated me like a child till she died when I was fifty years old. However, the sense of "me" has remained the same from the time I remember, though I have grown from a child to an older man.

It is always the two of us in this cafe, except for today. Today I invited someone to join us. I don't know whether to call him a friend or just a passerby. I had bumped into him at the Metro station a few days ago and he immediately introduced himself as a Mystic. I was stumped. I have never met someone who said mysticism was their profession.

I thought this Mystic will help Maya and hence I invited him for tea.

I'm anxiously waiting for the Mystic and there he is. He waves at me and takes the third chair without any courtesy. Maya looks at me quizzically and perhaps saying "who the hell…?" I immediately turn to her and say "I want to introduce you to the Mystic. I invited him to join us for coffee and listen to what he does".

As if I have given him the cue, the Mystic starts off like a high-speed train. He speaks non-stop for 15 minutes till the Waiter comes and ask the Mystic if he would like to order something.

Once he ordered, Mystic turned to us and said, "I'm a tea leaf reader". "You mean you know the different kinds of tea leaves" asked Maya. Mystic laughed loudly and exclaimed "Oh you don't know what is tea leaf reading? I read the patterns created by the tea leaves at the bottom of the cup after we finish our tea and tell you your fortune" I can see Maya shifting uncomfortably in the chair. But I'm excited.

When we finished our tea, Maya turned around to the Mystic and said "Ok. Read my tea leaves" and handed the cup to the Mystic. For the first time that afternoon, silence fell on our table. The Mystic was peering into the cup, and we were staring at him.

After a few minutes, the Mystic started his non-stop talk explaining to Maya what the patterns mean and what it the future seen from these patterns. I started feeling very embarrassed by the whole thing. But Maya was listening carefully and asking questions though with a skeptical look on her face.

Suddenly, the Mystic turned to me and said "There is only one of you here"

We have an eerie silence. I don't know what to respond. Maya got up and without even looking at me, walked away. I hurriedly paid the cheque, told the Mystic to wait and ran after Maya. I saw the Bus number 32 leaving the stop and I knew that Maya has left. I ran back to the table where we were sitting. The waiter was cleaning the table. I asked the waiter whether he saw the Mystic.

The Waiter looked a bit puzzled. He replied "Sir, you were alone at this table". I started feeling dizzy and realized that I'm standing on a ledge and the whole café is on a mountain slope. I can see the deep gorge below me.

Just then I feel a hand on my shoulder. I turn around and it is Maya. I just woke up! I woke up with a start. I was almost falling from a ledge and I got up. It was a dream and thankfully I'm still in my bed!

As I folded the sheets, I kept thinking whether the "falling from a ledge" in the dream was connected to my being at the edge of my bed? It could be that the "ledge" was a metaphor for the "edge" of the bed since the dream communication is using a symbolic language. Was my conscious mind giving me a message through the dream to turn over and maybe when I didn't, woke me up? Or is it a message from my unconscious mind that I'm on an edge in some aspects of my life and I need to be more careful?

I have been a regular visitor to that café along with Maya. I'm not sure whether it was a dream or I'm recalling something from my memory that I have tried to forget. The Mystic seem vaguely familiar, someone I have met and who tried to con me into buying something and I did!

I despise tea-leaf reading and such similar acts of fortune telling and in my dream, I seem to believe in it. Behind this façade of my confident self, lurks the fear of my own impermanence. Knowing that nothing is permanent is strangely fascinating and yet scary. Knowing the expiry date of permanency is the only thing I achieve from the fortune telling. That's not soothing either.

Mystic's statement at the end is still ringing in my ears "there is only one of you here". Perhaps the Mystic was telling me that he is a character in my dream and so was Maya, the Waiter, the café and everything. I was the only one present and the rest were all appearances in my mind.

In the dream world the objects and people are creations of our mind. It is like Tweedledee telling Alice "You'd be nowhere…..if that King was to wake, you'd go out -bang!-just like a candle" Unlike Alice, the person that I dreamed of knew that he was a dream character. Imagine if I knew that I don't exist except as a figment of your imagination!

I remember reading Sophie's World where Sophie is a figment of imagination in Hilde's mind and the world felt completely normal from her place. Towards the end of the book, we have Hilde opening her father's present for her birthday which is a book titled "Sophie's World". The book tells Sophie's story, and Hilde rapidly moves through the chapters. She realizes that Sophie got her birthday cards that were sent from her father, Sophie finds her silk scarf and her gold crucifix that was lost. Hilde becomes very confused, because she does not know how her father could have known it was lost. She becomes certain that Sophie actually exists. Like my Mystic who seem to know my mind, because he is in my mind, Sophie seem to know everything since Sophie is in Hilde's mind.

It is true that the waking world seem to follow some laws of nature and has an sense of coherence. The apple always fall down in the waking world and will never go up. In the dream world, I could be climbing a flight of stairs and land in the basement or a cave. So objects, space and time in dreams don't follow a pattern like in the waking world. In a dream, we could move from New York to London immediately and have events across many years happening in a few moments. I have experienced sleeping for an hour and the dreamtime spanned many years! Also in the dream, if I'm climbing a mountain, I can safely say that I'm not "really" climbing one since when I wake up, I wouldn't be sweating. However, if I'm thinking in a dream, can I say, I'm not thinking? In fact there are many people, including scientists and artists who claim that they thought about something or got an idea in their dream.

Let us say that we use a list of criteria to decide whether a particular experience is a waking one or in the dream. Like in the movie, Inception, Christopher Nolan introduces the totem of the spinning top to indicate whether the experience is real or in a dream. In the movie, the claim is made that if the spinning top starts to wiggle, it is real and if it continues spinning forever it is a dream. In the last scene of the movie, the top is spinning and just before we know whether it is starting to wiggle, the movie ends! Now the issue here is that the whole process of judging an experience using the criteria could also be in the dream. Hence how can we differentiate?

I remember a story that my grandmother used to tell me when I was a child. As the story goes, King Janaka was sleeping in his royal bedroom and he had a dream. In his dream, his kingdom was attacked and captured by a rival king and King Janaka was forced into exile. He was shed of his royal garments and made to wear tattered clothes. He managed to run away and reach another kingdom. By then he was tired, and hungry from his long journey and he desperately wanted some food and water. He sees a soup kitchen where they were feeding the hungry and he joins the queue. When his turn comes to get the food, there was none left and he begs the man to offer him something. The serving person obliges and gets some scrap of food from the bottom of the pot and offers him in a bowl. As the King is about to eat the meal, a crow comes and takes the bowl away. He collapses to the ground and cries. King Janaka woke up crying in his royal bed. He was disoriented by this nightmare that he kept asking everyone he met "Was that dream real or is this real?" His courtiers couldn't give him a satisfactory answer till a wandering Monk came to his Palace. He said to the King "Oh King, you are not sure whether your exile was a dream or you are the exile who dreams that he is a king. However, in both the situations, you are sure about your presence. Hence, Oh King, the only reality is you alone" The message of the Monk is that only the Self is real. I don't know why my Granny told me that story when I was very young, or did she?

A dream is like a long drawn love affair. When it lasts, it seems so real and when it breaks, it seems like a dream. Our waking experience is no different either. From the present, the past does feel like a dream. Not necessarily a distant past, but even experiences from yesterday!

I experience wetness beneath my feet and see water spilled next to my bed. The bottle of water that I keep next to me has fallen down and the cap has slipped out spilling out water. So, the bottle was on the edge! I seem to be in a half-dream, half-awake state. I think I need a strong coffee to wake me up!

"What is real. How do you define real? If you're talking about what you can feel, what you can smell, what you can taste and see, then real is simply electrical signals interpreted by your brain. This is the world that you know. The world as it was at the end of the twentieth century. It exists now only as part of a neural-interactive simulation that we call the Matrix. You've been living in a dream world, Neo. This is the world as it exists today.... Welcome to the Desert of the Real"
Morpheus to Neo in Matrix

CHAPTER TWO

WAKING

Now that I have had a few sips of coffee, I feel fully awake. My mind is whizzing with thoughts about the waking world! The more I tell my mind to stop it and focus on what I need to do today, the more it runs away to bring strange thoughts! Sorry, did I say "I tell my mind?" That is not true. It is a part of the mind telling the other part of the mind! I'm just watching this.

I once remember climbing up to the attic in search of a box my mother thought she had kept there. It was pitch dark and I couldn't find the light switch. My mother was standing below and she asked me "Is that box there?" I couldn't say it is there nor I could say it isn't since all I could "see" was darkness. It sounds strange to write this – I could "see" darkness. Sometimes I feel the world is like that as well. We don't know whether it is really there or not there and all we could see is that we can't really see.

We experience the waking world through our five senses. We see, hear, smell, taste and touch. We see forms and shapes and the mind interprets them as an object. When we see a tree, the image of the tree is imprinted in our retina and a neural signal is transmitted to the Brain. Although we tend to think that our eyes faithfully report whatever is in front of us, the retina apparently records an imperfect and confusing image that is then rectified by the brain. I remember reading an article by a Neuroscientist that said that we don't see reality, we see a story that's created by us. This reinforces the old adage that "we see what we want to see". It looks like our brain unconsciously ends our perception of the world to meet our desires and expectations based on our past experiences.

Anyway, at that time my sense of sight was useless since I couldn't see anything. I was using my sense of touch to locate the light switch. I didn't answer my mother and went on groping the walls to find the light switch. After a couple of minutes, I hear her again "Are you there?" She asked. That was a surprising question but for which I had a definite answer- "Yes". Even though it was pitch dark and I couldn't see anything, including me, I could still say with conviction that I'm there. Maybe that is the only thing I can be sure of anytime, my presence.

Later I heard my Dad's voice saying "It may be at the right side corner". Damn. They seem to know the existence of something that I can't see. Now I replied "Wait. I need to find the light switch first".

At last, I switched on the light and like my father said, I found a box in the right side corner of the attic. Was it always there or it appeared when I saw it? Our common belief is that the world is there waiting for us to perceive. I had kept my mobile phone by the side of my bed when I went to sleep and when I woke up, it was there.

However, there are others who believe that the world appears only when we perceive it and yet others who believe that the perceiver, perceived and the act of perception emerge together.

Imagine a child from a remote village who has never seen a movie in a theatre or a television. You take the child to experience a movie in a theatre. On your way to that theatre, you tell the child that a movie is a set of images that is projected on a screen at a particular speed so that a story can be told. Imagine that the movie had already started when you and that child entered the hall. It was dark and the screen was bright with moving pictures. The child gets engrossed in watching the movie. She cries when characters cry, she laughs with them and imagines herself out there as a character. You also get engrossed, laugh and cry like the child, but in the back of your mind, you know it is a movie. After a while, she turns to you and asks "where is the screen?" You will not be able to get the child to see the screen because one sees pictures wherever one looks. When the movie is over and the lights come back, you can show the screen.

Like that child, we enter life when the movie is already playing. The world is there, people are there and we enter that world and start playing our part in the best way we know. Like that child, we don't see what is behind all this as long as the movie of life is playing. When the child knows that there is a screen behind it all, she will still stay captivated by the movie and her life with all the characters. But she knows that it is only a movie. When it is over, we can say "we had a good time and now it is over".

Anyway, to cut the long story short, I found the box, brought it down and after examination, my mother said it was not the one that she was looking for. I don't remember whether we ever found that mysterious box till she died. I also never asked her what was in that box either. I don't even know whether the box she and my father imagined were the same or different. Were there two boxes or one? Did both of them ever exist in reality? I will never know the answers to these questions.

We do see different things and/or see the same things differently. Then the Psychologist in me says "We see images rather than real objects or people. What we see is coloured by our beliefs, prejudices, assumptions and past experiences. The eyes get an inverted image of the object or person, but when the mind reads what the eyes see, it is given a form, name and meaning based on the past knowledge of the mind". But then, there is no one in the world who is not coloured by her own beliefs etc. But for every her, him and me the world we experience in the waking world is real.

If I take the neurologist, psychologist and mystic arguments together, then it appears to me like this. The world is an appearance of a zillion objects. I'm the subject that is experiencing these objects. Reality is the construction of that experience in my mind.

I look at my calendar and I see that I'm in workshops and meetings the whole day. The pandemic has meant that all work happen in the virtual world. I don't meet my clients in person but see images of them on my screen. I wonder how they are in the "real world"? I believe that people present themselves differently on the screen. We never see ourselves when we meet others physically, but in the virtual world we can, like in a mirror. Hence we become hyper-aware about one's appearance, like when we are in front of a mirror. I also appear dressed up in a nice shirt and they don't see my boxer shorts!

I need to get ready soon. But I'm obsessed with thoughts and can't let it go. I put on my walking shoes and decided to think as I walk!

I see a Man walking a Dog coming towards me. As soon as they reach about 10 feet from me the Dog started to bark and wanted to jump on me! The Man struggled to hold back the Dog and said "Sorry" when they crossed me. The Dog continued its strange behaviour for another few seconds and was calm again. I also noticed them crossing the walker behind me and the Dog was calm and quiet! What did the Dog see? Did I appear like a Dog or a Cat ? I just looked at myself and touched my body to ensure that I'm the same person!

When people behave like that Dog and see things that a majority of us don't, we call that person delusional. I think we are all delusional in varying degrees and under different circumstances. I know that I behave like that Dog many times. I get emotional about things that I experience in the moment and later realise my folly. I colour all my experiences in my waking life with my memories, thoughts and feelings that I rarely experience an object or a person for what he/she is or what it is. Because the reality I'm seeing is based on name, form and attributes I'm giving to what I see rather than what is. Many of us do that and according to me, that is delusional too.

I returned home, showered and put together something for breakfast. I told Maya about my dream and she responded "I feel it is all a spaghetti. Maybe the real issue you may want to focus is the message of falling from the ledge". I told her that in a way I'm falling and in mid-air! I need to hit reality soon or I will go crazy with my thoughts.

I went through the first Zoom call like a split person. I had conflicting voices asking me to stay focussed on the call and to stay focussed on my thoughts triggered by my dream. The fight ended with the call! Thankfully my next call got cancelled and I had an hour.

There seem to be a clear split within me around the question of appearance and presence. This split is there in the world as well. The scientific approach suggests that the world is real since everything follows the laws of space and time. However, there is an alternate view offered by the quantum physicists who suggest that the reality is subjective since what is observed is based on the observer. The oriental traditions of Tao, Buddhist and Hindu thought say that the world is an appearance and we considering this appearance as real is the cause of all suffering.

The Sun appears to rise in the East every morning, travel from east to west and set in the West. It appears very real though we all know that it is the Earth that is moving and not the Sun. But imagine for a second, if it was indeed the Sun that was moving and not the Earth, will we see anything differently? I don't think so. What appears will continue to be the same....the sun will rise in the east and set in the west! But this learning changes our perspective of what it means to be human in a small planet called Earth compared to the earlier belief that Earth was the centre of the Universe.

Our Earth is hurtling through space at 30kms per second and also rotating at 1000 kms per hour and yet we appear to be stable! Some of these things are unimaginable.

When I was a teenager, I was very taken in by the television series called "Cosmos" by Carl Sagan. I used to stay up at night and watch the stars and identify the constellations. Once a distant Uncle was visiting us and he was a professor of Astrophysics. One night, we were watching the sky together and he was explaining to me about big bang and black holes and so on. Then he said something that changed my perspective completely. He told me "the stars that you see in the sky tonight probably don't even exist". "How come?" I asked him and he replied "the light from the stars take millions of years to reach the earth and what you see today is how it was when the light left the star". He added "We will never see the stars of today, since their light will reach the earth millions of years after we have long gone". That was a difficult lesson to comprehend then, and even now.

This is the case about stars. The sunlight takes 499 seconds to reach the earth. We only see the Sun eight minutes in the past, we actually see the past of everything in space. We even see our closest companion, the Moon, 1 second in the past. The further an object is from us the longer its light takes to reach us since the speed of light is finite and distances in space are really huge.

What about objects that I see on earth, what about people? Neuroscientists say that our brains take anywhere between 200 milliseconds to few seconds to recognise an object or a person based on prior information being available. So recognising Maya will takes me 200 milliseconds and recognising someone whom I haven't met for years might take a few seconds and even minutes. Of course, these figures are contested since data measured with instruments under experimental conditions are different from ordinary life experiences. But I'm not interested in the accuracy of the measurements. I'm interested in the fact that there is an interval of time between the instance when our senses get data to the time our brain makes meaning. Hence all that we recognise in our brain is from the past. The "now" that we perceive died a few milliseconds ago.

It is almost lunch time now. Maya is waiting for me to have lunch together. I need to go down to the Kitchen. After lunch, we plan to drive from our Goa home to our Mumbai home. Driving from Goa to Mumbai is always a pleasurable experience, though it can take 12 hours of driving. This time we have decided to take it easy and drive slowly with breaks on the way to stop, pause and see the world and people that we pass through.

"Lead us from the unreal to the real. Lead us from darkness to light. Lead us from death to immortality"
Brihadaranyaka Upanishad 1.3.28

CHAPTER THREE

TRAVELING

The best part of the drive between Goa and Mumbai is filling up one's senses with the freshness of air, the smell of dried cow dung, see the soft green coloured fields of sugarcane and the taste the local delicacies in the roadside stalls. After an hour of driving, we left the highway and went through narrower roads lined with lush green fields, hills and rivers. We stopped the car after we had climbed up a small hillock to take a stretch break and also enjoy nature. In front of us is a vast expanse of fields as far as the eye can see. A gentle breeze is caressing our faces and just below us is a field of bright red peppers being invaded by yellow birds who seem to enjoy the spicy stuff. The smell of the ripened peppers is strong, sweet and alluring. The birds are constantly chirping a short whistle like sound as they continued their busy work of eating. These sounds filled the whole valley below in a constant buzz. I went to a nearby shop adjacent to the sugarcane field and ordered two glasses of sugarcane juice. The man who prepared the juice had a manual crusher where he crushed the sugarcane and the juice was collected in an dark red earthen bowl. He then squeezed two lemons to the sugarcane juice and served us in large glasses. The sweet and tangy taste of the juice opened up all my taste buds asking for more.

This feels like heaven, right? Being with Maya in this gorgeous land, watching the small yellow birds chipping on the red peppers below, with the expanse of the vast sugarcane fields beyond, drinking the farm to mouth fresh, sweet sugarcane juice. My body is happy and so are my senses and my mind also seem to be at ease and not anxious about the route ahead, for a change! Yet my intellect is getting restless.

We experience the world through our five senses. It is a fact that our senses have limitations, both in terms of range and intensity. For example, we can hear sounds in a frequency range from 20 Hertz to 20 Kilohertz. Sounds that are above or below this range is not detected by the human ear. Further, we lose high frequency sensitivity when we grow older, the upper limit in average adults is 15-17 kilo hertz. Similar is the case with our other senses like sight, smell, taste and touch. Hence my intellect is asking, What am I missing here?

Our senses only sense the world around us and they don't interpret the world. The eyes only see forms and shapes. When we see the fields, we say "I am seeing a tall sugarcane field" The interpretation that it is a "field", it is "sugarcane" and it is "tall" are all made in my mind based on past experiences and knowledge acquired about sugarcane fields. In case someone is seeing a sugarcane field for the first time, in his mind, he will wonder what are these tall, vertical objects across a vast space. It is also possible that we "think" it is Sugarcane plantation because our memory says it so. We could actually be wrong here. Similarly, if we see the same field in fading light or in darkness, we might interpret it for something else altogether.

We also say that the Sugarcane has brownish trunk and green leaves. But our eyes don't actually see any colour and nor does objects have colour! Our eyes only see light and our brain translates that into a particular colour based on the colour the object reflects in that light. It is a fact that our senses exclude rather than identify. For example, we don't see red color, but our nervous system eliminates all other colors except red. However, in yellow light the same red apple will appear as orange since the red is now eliminated by our nervous system.

The National Geographic Channel has a serial called "Welcome to Earth" (hosted by the Actor Will Smith) where they explore the existence of colours that we don't see, the odours that we don't smell, the sounds that we don't hear and so on. According to them, there is a whole world out there that is beyond our senses.

Imagine a Botanist and a Poet are together and watching the same phenomenon, like me and Maya. My mind is that of a Botanist. I will analyse what I see, classify the things I see into different names, forms and utilities and possibly its age and other characteristics. I miss the aesthetics, the beauty and the awesomeness of my sights. Maya on the other hand has a Poet's mind. She will just be awestruck by the beauty and intensity of the place and imagines how the various elements of nature -the peppers, the birds, the sugarcane fields and even the man who crushes the sugarcane are all connected in the web of life. She will even listen to the sound of that place, the aromas and touch the air. Our senses pick up the same forms and shapes and yet our minds generate completely different experiences for us to feast on.

Yet, we believe that we heard whatever is there to hear and saw whatever is to be seen! Funnily, each one of us will feel so, though what appeared to each one us is different from what is.

We need both the views, analytic and aesthetic to take in everything that our senses have to offer and completely experience. However, completeness of an experience is not an evidence for the reality of that. We humans have a great capacity to experience a phenomenon even when we know that it is an illusion. I could be watching a movie and use both the analytical and aesthetic view and immerse myself in that experience knowing very well that it is only a movie.

Is it that I see the beautiful scene because it is there, or I see it and therefore it is? In other words, does the presence of the scene appear to me or is it my presence that makes the scene appear to me? I have this doubt because what I'm seeing is in my mind and not really what is. Any process of knowledge (in this case, sugarcane fields) requires a knower (in this case me), the thing to be known (in this case the scene) and the process of knowing (in this case by the process of seeing). All the three must be present for the experience of knowledge to occur and that happens together. When I'm not there, there is no sugarcane field.

It was the philosopher Locke, I believe, who proposed that the world that is experienced by our senses is never real. He asked the question "Is the world inside my mind an accurate picture of what the physical world really is, like a copy?" He answers that we can never form a complete picture of an object in our minds that matches the object itself as it really is. Our mind can only create a representation of reality. In order to solve this problem, Locke suggested that we identify what he called as "primary qualities" of an object like the size, shape etc. and objectively measuring them will help us to create a reliable information about the object. However, there are also "secondary qualities" that cannot be objectively measured. The secondary qualities depend on the Subject who is experiencing the Object. While we can all agree on the size and colour of a lemon, the experience of sourness that one experiences is subjective and cannot be objectively determined. Imagine, a pool of water kept at a particular temperature (primary quality) and two people jump into that pool, one emerging from a hot shower and another from a cold shower. The water appears warm in one case but freezing in the other, though the temperature of the pool remain unchanged.

What we see (or hear, taste, touch, or smell) can be definable in an objective manner, but the experience of what we see is entirely subjective. When I hit my toe on the leg of the dining table the other day, my nerve fibres shot a message to my spinal cord, sending neurotransmitters to the brain and that activate my limbic system. This is the easy problem of consciousness since we do have an explanation for all this. But how come all that was accompanied by an agonising flash of pain? And what is pain, anyway? My first-person experience (technically called "qualia") of pain cannot be explained in an objective manner. This is called the "hard problem" of consciousness by the cognitive scientist, David Chalmers.

I hold this perspective that when we see a flower, we experience a "flower-ness". In reality, we experience existence or *"is-ness" and* superimpose *"such-ness"* to it. Hence "flower-ness" is a superimposition of the object called flower on its existence. That existence is nothing but our Self. *In every experience of seeing, hearing, smelling, touching, tasting — there exists one "is" and that is our Self.*

The sun started going down below the hills and the light started to change. The pale green fields looked greener now and the birds just disappeared leaving the red peppers alone. The breeze seemed to stop as if waiting for the sun to set. It is now time to leave this tranquil surrounding and continue the drive.

Even after we crossed a few miles from that hillock, the scene remained in my mind as if I was looking at a picture.? Is the picture in my memory real or am I imagining now about a place that doesn't exist like that anymore? If I go back to that place now, will it exist the way I see in my mental picture?

Maya seemed to sense my daydreaming and asked, "Do you want me to take over the driving?". I shrugged, got the message, and said "sure, at the next gas station".

After an hour of driving, I saw a petrol station by the side of the road and stopped. I got out of the car and asked the attendant whether they have a washroom. He pointed to where it was. The toilet was in semi-darkness, and I opened the door and immediately closed it because I thought I saw a snake! Maya was just behind me, and she was surprised by my action. "What's the problem?" She enquired and I realized that my heart was beating faster and there was fear within. "I think there is a snake inside" I said. She just pushed past me, opened the door, and switched on the light. There was a cloths rag used to mop the floor that I mistook as a snake. Seeing that cloths rag made me feel both relieved and a bit sheepish having made a mistake.

We used the toilet, filled the tank and this time Maya took the wheel. I was still shaken by my experience of seeing a snake when it was not there. I realized in that moment when I mistook that rag for a snake, my fear overshadowed my intellectual capacity to think. I experienced fear which was real though there was no real snake. Maya changed that reality in me by switching on the light! The appearance of the snake that I thought of as presence was destroyed by her action. Not only that I realized my error of false identification, but I also saw what was there. I felt liberated from my error but felt sheepish for having been erroneous!

The rag was the reality behind the snake. The appearance of snake cannot be there without the presence of the rag. Similarly, the world that we experience is an appearance and the presence behind that is the reality. The snake requires the rag for its appearance, but the rag doesn't need the snake for its presence.

The light that Maya switched on removed the illusion of the snake and revealed the reality of the cloth rag. But how can one say that the cloth rag is real too? Likewise, the beautiful, vast sugarcane fields that I visited earlier. Was that real? Since it was a pleasant experience unlike the false snake, I didn't backout from it and stayed there soaking it in. Since I didn't backout and Maya also didn't do anything to change the situation like switching on the light, that appearance felt like presence!

The Indian Vedantic traditions speak about three planes of existence. The first plane is called the plane of illusory existence. The mirage can be said to be non-existent since the water we perceive to be there doesn't really exist at all. Our ignorance makes us believe the existence of water and when we gather knowledge that it is a mirage, the delusion will disappear. However, the mirage will not disappear from our eyes even when we know that it is unreal! Sometimes we even tend to forget that it is a mirage and say "look, there is water". Even the dream I had about falling from the ledge was like the mirage, it was just my creation without any basis or underlying reality.

While the mirage and the dream is recognised by us as illusionary, there are other forms of existence that are close to these illusions but we take them for granted in our lives. For example the entire set of alphabets, numbers, algebra, geometrical shapes are abstractions and don't really exist but we will struggle to live without them. Even the concept of time and space are abstractions that help us to make sense of the worldly existence.

Beyond the illusory world is the world of empirical reality which has subject and object -me, the individual and the world around me. Time, space and causality are also part of this world. It is difficult to say whether this world is also like the illusion of the mirage or the dream, though it seem to be based on a fundamental reality. Vedanta calls it as *"maya"* which is neither an appearance nor presence. I remember a Vedanta teacher give the example of gold ornaments. There could be a necklace, a tiara and a ring all made from gold. We give them the names, they have different forms and shapes and uses. But in reality they are nothing but gold. If you take the gold away, there is no ornament. In this example, the ornaments represent appearance and gold is the fundamental reality or presence.

The independent existence of a mirage and the empirical world, both of which are due to a certain causal condition, ceases once the causal condition changes. The causal condition is our own ignorance where we divide the subject (me) and the object (world). Ancient wisdom says that once we transcend this divide and experience it as one, we will recognise the ultimate presence which is consciousness and everything including one's body-mind complex is an appearance of the same.

I was jolted out of my thoughts as a car crossed us with loud music blaring. Looks like they want everyone to be alert to their music. Maya is focussed on the road and we are approaching the city of Pune where we intend to stay overnight at a friend's place.

We enter the Katraj road tunnel and when we emerge on the other side, the lights of Pune city come into my view. Just before the tunnel, the world around was mountainous, dark and without a single building, and after a mile of tunnel, a big metropolis unfolds before one's eyes. It is almost like the city was waiting for me to be seen, all lit up.

'Reality is merely an illusion, albeit a very persistent one.'
Albert Einstein

CHAPTER FOUR

PARTYING AND AFTER

We stop at my friend's home in Pune for the evening and we have reached at the right time. The party is on! Many of our friends are there and the evening is starting to warm up as the drinks flowed along with music and dance. Most of the conversations were around health, exercise and diets indicating the age group that is present! I'm sure that if the group is a bunch of twenty year olds, the topics of conversation would be completely different and even the music and dance! It will be an interesting research to record sounds at a party and from there identify the demographics of the group partying.

A couple arrived and everyone turned to them to say hello and hug. I was happy to see them again since I had known them 10-12 years ago and subsequently lost touch. At that time

I thought they were on the verge of separating and now they look like two love birds! Both of them have changed their appearance completely. He used to look like the typical corporate honcho, clean shaven, crop cut and in smart casuals or business suits. Now he had long hair tied into a pony tail, a salt and pepper beard and wore capris and a t-shirt! She used to be this flamboyant woman, talkative, flirting, who electrified every party by her energy and presence. Now she looked quiet, speaking softly, having one to one conversations, slow and tired.

I meet them and after exchanging some pleasantries, I said "you both have changed a lot" and they both responded almost in unison "No, no. You never saw this side of us". I felt sheepish and a bit put off when I heard that. However, my mind is overworking now on these questions, "why did they deny that they have changed?" and "Why did they say that I didn't see that side of them?"

It is true that I had stereotyped them to a particular category of people and more importantly, I believed, that the way they appeared to me is how they are. I never imagined that there could be another side to them that is different from what I experienced even when I know at some level that we are all capable of whatever we want to be. It is also true that I had also changed from the way I was to how I'm now. Still it is difficult to accept the changing nature of all and the impermanence of all phenomenon – objects and people, that I experience. Including, my own experience of myself!

The "other side" of them that I experience now was present even when I saw them a decade ago. It is just that I didn't see it and I chose to see only what I wanted to see. It is me who has changed and not them. Here too I'm in the danger of stereotyping them again into this pony tailed casual man and the quiet, tired woman. In the pony tailed man lies the seed of the corporate honcho and in the quiet woman also lies the seed of energy and flamboyance.

I wonder where the seeds of my judgement are. I judge everything I see and put them in nice pigeon holes so that I have a certain understanding of the world. I judge objects and people (technically both are objects with me as the subject) into good- bad, beautiful- ugly and so on when there is no such value attached by nature. There is no beautiful flower and a good person as far as nature is concerned. Nature says "It is", it is existence, nothing more and nothing less.

I think there are two things to consider here, one is my objectifying what is essentially a subjective experience and secondly, the reality of impermanence that my mind refuses to accept. Objective reality is what we can measure through our observations – size, weight, shape, spin, charge etc. Even these are subjective at sub-atomic levels as per Quantum physics because the measurement depends on the Observer, the Subject. In Objective reality, there is no judgement involved, just data. I might hold two mangoes in my hand and say one is heavier or larger than the other. This can be verified using a ruler and a weighing scale. When I bite into both the mangoes, I experience the flavours and form an opinion which one is better than the other. This is a judgement that is subjective. However, I tend to give the same value to this subjective judgement like the objective data.

There is another level of subjective experience that is even more subtle. This is the experience of experiencing, also called first person experience or 'qualia". The way I experience myself when I bite into a sweet mango is different from the way I experience me when I bite into a sour one. This is not about the mango nor about the sensation of sourness or sweetness in my tongue. It is about experiencing me in that process. I experience the delightful me in the sweetness of the mango and the disappointed me in the sourness. This may be opposite for a person who loves sourness and hates sweetness! Hence I say, "I love the sweet mango and don't like the sour one" instead of saying "I like the delighted me and not the disappointed me and in order to generate that experience of the delighted me again and again, the sweet mango is what I turn to".

When I experienced the couple at the party, it was not so much the objective data of how they were dressed or behaved, it was also not about how I interpreted that data in my mind. It was about how I experienced me in that process. Now I can say that I experienced me as happy to see them and nothing else mattered. However, I didn't at all focus on that inner experience of me and acted on their appearance and behaviour that I saw and judged. So I missed my own presence and consequently theirs and I ended up making a mess of myself!

The host offered all of us a box of Ladoos, a common sweet in India. I said no to it and she said "Sankar this is Tirupati Prasad" (the sweet was offered to the deity in the temple of Tirupati and then offered to devotees). Suddenly the common ladoo changed to a sacred offering. I said "oh, ok" and took a small piece of it. One can't say no to a temple offering, even though one can to a sweet.

I'm thinking about my decision to partake the sweet after I was told that it was an offering to God. Somehow it changed the way I saw that sweet or in other words, the sweet changed its appearance for me because it touched some unconscious part of me that still holds the sacredness of temple offerings.

I had a similar experience with the Indian national flag also. I once had a small flag that was pasted to the dashboard of my car. After a few months, the flag holder came unstuck and I had a lot of difficulty in deciding how to dispose the flag. It was just a small tricoloured piece of cloth but it had the design of the national flag and I didn't want to do anything that will be disrespectful to the flag. I wouldn't have thought twice to throw away anything else.

Every object has a name, a form and a utility. We call a flower as a rose or a lily, even add an attribute like a "white rose". The same rose has a form that distinguishes it from other flowers and an ornamental utility. However, the flower acquires a different name and utility if it is part of a bouquet, offered to someone you love or presented at the altar. We look at it differently though it remains the same. It is fascinating how our internal associations change the nature of the object that appear.

Today happens to be the spring festival of colours, Holi. The Hosts bring some "gulal" (coloured powder that is anointed on each other's cheeks as part of the festival celebrations). All of us anointed the colours on each other's faces in a civilised way indicating that we have grown old! If we were a few years younger, we would have a riot of colours plastered on each other! The Hosts now bring glasses filled with a drink called "Bhang" (made from Indian Hemp flowers mixed in Milk). Bhang is a hallucinating drink that is very much part of the Holi celebrations like throwing the gulal at each other. I drank a glass of that drink and had Maya's too when she offered it to me after a sip.

Gulal and Bhang completed changed the appearance of the party. The initial stiffness and appropriateness started loosening. The splash of colours seem to make us appear vibrant, younger and free. After initial reluctance to have colours spoiling our dresses, people are enjoying the new look in them and others. The Bhang made us less inhibited and even the few strangers at the party started appearing like close friends to me. There was more laughter, singing and dancing. I lost all track of time and even space. The Bhang in me generated this thought to sing! A friend offered to video record my performance. That was my last memory of the day and then I found myself being woken up by Maya the next morning, almost mid-day since the wall clock showed 11.15 AM!

During breakfast, the friend who had taken the video of my singing offered to show me what he had recorded. I thought the video will show me singing some song in a voice that I will be ashamed of….but it turned out be something else. I had climbed halfway up a coconut tree and swinging wildly and there was no singing! I remember singing and even the song that I thought I sang, but the video recording shows otherwise. The video is empirical data whereas my memory of my singing is an internal experience that could be illusional. From a common perspective, my internal experience is seen as false and the video is real. My mind was probably playing tricks with me since the neurons in my Brain went crazy because of the two glasses of Bhang. However, my mind refuses to believe so, since it has "recorded" in its video a memory of my singing a song!

I asked my friend and others who were there whether it was true that I didn't sing, and they agreed. My friend who shot the video went on to add that I asked him to shoot the video when I was swinging from the tree! As we got into the car, I was shaking my head, still unable to reconcile the empirical data with my inner experience. Maya, patted me on my back and said "You know, the whole thing including the party could be an appearance. Maybe you should just stay off such stuff"

It is well known that hallucinating substances generate experiences that are "unreal". But how did my Brain trick me into think that I was singing when I was swinging from a tree? You might say I was seeing things that other people didn't, like when we look at a cloud, and see faces in them.

Hallucinations are defined as sensory experiences that appear real but are creations of the mind. Isn't that true for every sensory experience? The way I will experience the redness of a Rose might not be the same for anyone else. In fact, studies show that we see things in different shades and hues and if we have colour blindness, we don't see that colour at all. We seem to have a range of "normal" where we give allowance to difference of perception between individuals. This "normal" is breached under the influence of drugs or any other altered states like hypnosis or a psychotic episode. When that altered state persists, we call them "crazy".

Unfortunately, the "normal" itself is an appearance and not real.

Many years ago, I read about Plato's Allegory of the Cave. According to Plato's allegory, the way we understand things around us and the way we lead our lives is actually not based on truth or presence. Plato describes this condition of believing in appearances by depicting humans as prisoners in a cave. These prisoners are sitting facing a wall, bound in chains, with a fire between them and the wall, which makes shadows fall on the wall. These shadows are what form the "reality" for them because that is what the fellow prisoners or the ones before them conveyed. Generations come and go and the prisoners continue to lead the same unaware and limited lives in the dark caves until one of the prisoners finally starts questioning. This bondage to the walls is a metaphor for human senses that limit us; we believe whatever we see and hear but once one can rise above that, we break free. In the movie, Matrix, Morpheus brings Neo out of his "cave" of everyday existence, they do it in a manner analogous to Plato's Analogy of the Sun, in which "the sun is a metaphor for the nature of reality and knowledge concerning it," and the eyes of the fearful few forced out of their cave need some time to adjust to it.

I remember the red and blue tablets that Morpheus offers Neo in the movie. Neo has a choice to take the blue tablet that takes him to the "normal reality" or the red one that allows him to embrace the "really real". When one "unplugs" from the illusion-generating Matrix, a longer journey toward that really-real reality awaits. This is a take on what the ancient traditions called empirical or transactional reality and the ultimate truth.

John Wheeler, the famous Physicist once said "Useful as it is under ordinary circumstances to say that the world exists 'out there' independent of us, that view can no longer be upheld"

Hallucinations remind us that the mind that leads us to discover truth can also lead us to perceive a make believe world, because the neurological machinery in our brain is not fully reliable, and there is something beyond that we haven't understood yet. Navigating this difference is the challenge of living.

If the hallucination that I had was a weird perception, then a perception is also nothing but a controlled hallucination. I maybe hallucinating all the time, but in a controlled way so that I will be seen as normal. Anil Seth, a neuroscientist said "we are all hallucinating all the time. When we all agree on our hallucination, we call it reality".

I will try to keep remembering that reality always seems real. Even when I mess it up!

My thoughts were interrupted when Maya turned to tell me that we are dropping by to visit a couple who recently had a baby. She wants to stop at a gift store and pickup something for the baby before we visit them. I'm still a bit lost in my explorations around hallucinations and I just nod. She parked the car and asked me to stay in the car while she quickly shopped. I said yes happily since I didn't want to let go the last of my thoughts around my hallucinating experience!

One thing I have noted in hallucinating experiences is the absence of time and space. So too in dreamless deep sleep when the mind shuts down completely. Time is generally defined as the gap between two sequential observed instances of experiences. I have one thought and then another and the gap between these thoughts is elapsed time. When there is no experience, like in deep sleep, or when the Brain forgets to keep track of the gap between experiences, as in hallucinations, time as a phenomenon disappears.

Similar with space too. Space is the gap between two simultaneously observed experiences. This is possible if what is simultaneously observed is in the same realm of experience. In a hallucinated state, like the one where one experience was singing and the other was swinging from a tree, they are not in the same realm of reality even though they might be simultaneous. Hence space disappears.

It is fascinating that objects create space when we experience them and sequential experiences of the same object create time. When a car comes too close to mine, I become aware of the space (or the lack of it) between us and when I see that same car come close to us again, I sense time. When objects themselves could be appearances, time and space also are no different.

The cognitive scientist, Donald Hoffman says "Evolution has shaped us with perceptions that allow us to survive. But part of that involves hiding from us the stuff we don't need to know. And that's pretty much all of reality, whatever reality might be" He conceptualises, based on his simulations using evolutionary game theory, that species that see reality as real are less likely to survive than those that see what is "fit for survival" as real. "Truth is not needed to stay alive" Says Hoffman.

Maya's knocking the car window brought me back to this space and time! She is carrying a gift wrapped thing and a bouquet of roses. We are now ready to visit the baby.

"I never change, only the experience of I changes"
Deepak Chopra

CHAPTER FIVE

PRETENDING

We reach the home of the baby and such a cute baby she is! She is snuggled to her Mother and I asked her if I can hold her. She said "she is just a month old, so just hold her neck carefully". I happily take the baby and rock her and soon enough Maya wants her too.

Baby is a month *old*! I thought I will be called *old* at my age!. The moment we are born, we start aging. The baby will soon be one year old and a few years old thereafter. This cute baby will soon be a brat and then a young girl, a woman and perhaps a mother and a granny in her old age. Her appearances will change, her mind too, but will she become someone else? Today she is "cute". Can she remain that "cute" even if I see her many years later?

I'm fascinated by the creation of this baby. Does this baby know that she has left the safety of her Mother's womb and she is present in this world? Does the world that you and I know, exist for her? The baby has been given a name by her parents, does she like her name? Does she know that she is one month old and that she is a girl child?

I don't know the answer to these questions and maybe there are studies done in this area. However I believe that there is one thing She knows – that she exists. I can't prove it in any manner but this has been my experience from the time I remember me. This was true when I was young, middle-aged and now a bit older. This was true in whatever mental state I was. I always knew I exist and that was the only thing that I'm certain about.

I remember my mother always called me by my baby name even when I was in my forties! Not only did she call me by that name, at times she treated me like that too! She refused to change how she saw me despite my changes in appearance. I believe now, that she saw me very apart from how I showed up in the world.

I'm told that I was born on the first of January. Sometimes I think my parents found it convenient to put my birthdate as January 1 because I don't have a birth certificate to prove it!. They went more by the Indian calendar and astrology rather than the Julian calendar. But, let us look at it more closely. Am I really born on that date? Or was I born when I was conceived? Did I not exist in part in my father's sperm or my mother's ovum even before I was conceived? I believe that something cannot be born out of nothing. Hence I was existing in an unmanifest way (unmanifest from our perspective of form) and at birth, I manifested as this person. So too this Baby, she was there, always there. She is now seen in the name and form that I can call as a "Baby".

The baby is now placed in the cradle and she is happily stretching her hands and legs. I offer her my finger and she holds it and gives a smile. I don't know whether she smiled at me or just smiled…but it doesn't matter. I played with the baby for a while and soon enough she started to cry and her Mother took her to nurse.

I'm wondering how the baby sees this world and makes meaning. The baby might have a completely different experience of appearances and presence. But she is born into an already interpreted world without having a choice. It's like she walked into a movie which is already playing and the plot is unravelling. She is expected to become one more character. I remember my daughter used a gibberish language to describe her experiences and we corrected her. We made her say "apple" when she called that fruit something strange. Once me and my wife spoke about a possibility that she might be speaking a language that she spoke in her previous birth and we dump it as gibberish since we don't know that. Our need to make her see the world like we do prevailed over our curiosity to know her gibberish. Now she speaks our language!

We generate ideas in the baby about what is desirable and attractive that one needs to go towards and what is repulsive and undesirable that one needs to avoid. She then develops a polarised view of good and bad, right and wrong, that shapes her beliefs about herself and the world. I was remembering *Mowgli* in *Jungle Book* and how this kid developed a completely different worldview because he was brought up by a pack of wolves. Not just that, he also developed skills to converse with animals, run like them and even behave like them. Of course this was just the imagination of Kipling and we don't really know if such a kid ever was. But this makes me realise that so much of our sense of reality is pumped into us as children by our parents and teachers. I wish this baby sees the world with fresh eyes, untainted by us.

There is so much that we carry as our presence but those are really just appearances. For example, this baby has a name given to her. She will grow up taking this borrowed identity and call herself that. Same goes with language, nationality, religion, gender stereotypes and many others. This baby is also given the knowledge that someone is her mother, father and maybe her brother or cousin. These relationships become "family" and take the appearance of being sacred, like the example I had about the Tirupati Ladoos. If I take this baby to my home now and give her another name and bring her up, she will hold that as her identity. The same goes for her relationships and all other borrowed identities.

All these are acquired or superimposed on the self and doesn't actually belong to the self, like a crystal appears red against a red background without actually having that colour. This baby is like that crystal and we are too. All that we acquire as our identity is just an appearance and none of it is real. Unfortunately, this Baby will go through the same process that I have gone through, albeit most of humanity- believing that the acquired name, religion, language etc. is my real self and the ignorance that all this were actually superimposed on me by others. Once we get that insight, we want to strip ourselves and transcend beyond all superimpositions. However, it takes a lifetime (or many lifetimes!) to discard all that one has acquired and to discover one's real presence.

Some children from the neighbourhood came in to play with the baby. After a few minutes, they lost interest in the baby and started playing among themselves. I joined their game of hide and seek. It is now my turn to close my eyes and the children go hiding in the different rooms. I open my eyes and see a young boy behind the dining table. I go there and touch him and say "I found you". He has his eyes closed and he responds "I'm not here". Maya said to me "Hey, he is pretending that he is not there. You pretend too". I also pretended that he is not there and went in search of the other kids.

The words of this Boy "I'm not here" reverberated in my mind as I sipped some coffee and stared out of the window. Maya was busy chatting with her friend catching up on all the news about each other and all their family and friends. I remember growing up like that Boy when I had three imaginary friends with whom I pretended to have conversation and play games. I remember an Uncle whom I hated for some reasons and whenever he visited I tried to avoid him. However my Mother insisted that I bow before him in respect since he is my Uncle. I hated it, but pretended to be good, bowed quickly and ran away! I was pretending to be nice to him and more importantly I was pretending to be a "good boy".

I remember reading a humorous story of a child who thought she was a cat and refused to come out of her home because she was afraid that the dogs will chase her. She was met by a Psychotherapist who showed her a real cat and asked her if she resembled a cat in any way. She responded to the Psychotherapist "I know that I don't look like a cat. But can you tell that to the dog?" That kid pretended in all her innocence, but don't we all do it all the time, even as adults?

It is often said to someone who is anxious to make a good impression that "You don't have to pretend to be someone else. You are fine just the way you are". But I remember how I sometimes pretend to be a suave and sophisticated gentleman when I'm none of that. Selling myself to get a job or a consulting assignment also involved some pretension. One area where I have tried to pretend and failed is to be a charmer!

Pretence is a phenomenon we experience in nature as well. The classic colouration of the chameleon to match its surroundings is a pretence *to avoid being seen as what one really is.* We do that too. I remember the first time I was abroad with a group of 30 odd Europeans. I wished so much that I had a lighter skin every time someone took a photograph! I couldn't change my colour like the Chameleon but I could pretend to be an European in my dressing style, manners and even my way of communication! Later I realised futility of pretending and that I'm really proud of my Indian roots. From then on, I just let me be present as me.

Pretension could be in ways to mask the lesser or greater aspects of oneself. The Superhero's in the Hollywood movies always pretend to merge with the "normal" and bring in their superpowers only under a mask or a costume. The costume hides the "normal" person that most people are acquainted with. We play ourselves small in order to get accepted, loved and sometimes to gather sympathy. We could also pretend ourselves to be much larger than what we really are, leading to what psychologists call an "imposter syndrome" -an experience of feeling like a phony, with the fear of being found out as a fraud.

I'm tired of people who pretend to be this perfect person with a perfect partner leading a perfect life. I wish we can just be present and not have to appear to be someone that we are not. Maybe then the scars of imperfections will actually make us beautiful, unique and very relatable to others.

We create an appearance of ourselves not just to the world, but even for ourselves when we start to grow from a baby to an infant and later on to adulthood. We pull wool over our eyes and even start believing what we started as a role play.

There is an old Eric Clapton favourite of mine which goes like this *"Don't be pretending 'Bout how you feel, Don't be pretending, The love is real"*

The Baby here has no pretence whereas the four year old playing hide and seek does pretend. I'm fascinated to see how this little baby will develop her sense of "I" and along with that a "pretended I". From being an integral part of her mother's womb, she is an independent entity having her own body, mind and name. However, even now when she held my finger, she doesn't have the impression that she is holding someone else.

My presence of me in me remains constant despite all the changes in my body, mind and the world around me. This unchanging presence is my awareness. Then is it possible that beyond that unchanging presence, all appearance is a pretence? The baby's name is a pretence since it could have any other name. She will be told to behave, think, feel and even believe in a particular way as she grows up. At some deep level she knows that everything she is told to be is like a script described to an actor on stage or a movie. One has to remember the lines, behave "as if" you are that character and pretend to get impacted by events there even when we know that it is all an appearance.

One of the actors who played a central character in a long running play was asked about how he managed to live his life outside the stage. He had to pretend to be that character every evening for the play and when he left the theatre he had to revert back to his personality in life. He replied " I had real trouble with this in the beginning. Playing that character was like a dream. Sometimes we wake up from that dream and still continue the dream in the waking life. I had to get a whack from my wife or friends to wake up. Now, I really don't care since I realise that both in the play and in life, I'm playing a character. I just have to switch roles".

Interestingly, this baby is born when the play is already in progress. The other players in her play already know their scripts well and play their roles very well. The set is well defined, all the elements are named and the and She will be clumsy to begin with but she will learn. She will learn to play her role well till she wakes up and realises that, she is just playing a role in the drama of life that has been set for her!

This thought is so powerful that my body shook and I spilled some coffee in my shirt. I quickly went to the washroom to remove the stains from the shirt. I came out and Maya was ready to leave. She said "the baby has impacted you so much that you are lost in your own childhood". I said Yes and said quick goodbye to the Mother, blew a kiss to the baby and walked out.

The grass outside looks wet indicating that it has rained when we were there. I didn't see the rain, but I infer that there was rain since the effect of the rain (the grass is wet) is visible to me. This inference looks very logical though it is also possible that the Gardener might have watered the grass.

Much of the world we know is through inference. We look at people's faces and infer whether they are sad or happy. When we look at someone and say that person is happy or sad, our inference is based on "appearance", and we really don't know the "presence" of sadness or happiness in that person. The strange thing is that we believe our inferences to be true even when we know the possibility that they are pretending. At times both the person playing pretense and the person observing the same both know that it is just an appearance. Both believe it is part of a script.

Now there is a twist in the tale as well. The person who appeared sad recognizes his feelings at the first-person awareness. This feeling could be shame or elation at his pretended sadness. At times this awareness of the gap between the experienced feeling and the pretended one could confuse our minds about our own reality, making us delusional.

Now, I take the wheel and turn into the traffic leading to the highway to the city of Mumbai that is the home of "Bollywood" where, pretending well can help one become a billionaire. But before we reach the city, we are stopping over at a friend's hotel in Lonavala, a small town in the hills bordering the city of Mumbai.

"If you hold this feeling of 'I' long enough and strongly enough, the false 'I' will vanish leaving only the unbroken awareness of the real, immanent 'I', consciousness itself"
Ramana Maharshi

CHAPTER SIX

I AND NOT I

We take the exit from the highway and reach the outskirts of Lonavala. Once a peaceful village, it has become a buzzing tourist destination. People from Mumbai city visit Lonavala in droves to escape the heat, pollution and traffic jams and create them here! Today the roads are quiet since it is a Tuesday. People are busy trying to make a living in the city down there and will come here only by the weekend. We will anyway leave tomorrow!

We reach the gates of this quaint, homely looking Hotel with a scary name "Lion's Den" and my friend and owner was waiting for me in the Lobby. We hugged and he asked Maya whether we would like to eat something first. She said "I'm famished, but then we need to go and watch sunset"

We have some hot *batata vadas* (Potato cutlets fried in batter) with pao (small buns) along with some spicey chutney. It is difficult to stop at one and my mouth is still salivating after two vadas. I told my mind to stop and focused on the sweet tea. We put on our walking shoes and my friend also joined us in the trek to the sunset point. It is an easy walk at some places and steep inclines at others, and I find myself breathing heavily. I gather myself and keep up the pace with Maya and my friend till we reach the place.

The sunset point is on top of a 300-year-old Dam with a beautiful lake by the side. This lake supplies water to the city of Lonavala (it is no longer a village or town). My friend says it goes dry within six months after the rains since the number of residents and visitors have gone up many times from what was envisioned when the dam was built. I'm glad that I'm seeing the beautiful lake now, and not the dried patch of land if I had visited a few months later.

We are waiting for the sun to go down the horizon and set. Really? We know that the sun doesn't go anywhere, the earth turns in its axis, and it appears as if the sun is going down. But knowing the reality doesn't change the appearance. I can see the sun slowly going down.

Maya and my friend decide to sit in meditation and observe the sunset in silence. I decide to tell my wandering mind to focus on the new subject that is emerging for me, I and not I.

Our experiences can be divided into two dimensions, "I" experiences and "not I" experiences. The dress that I'm wearing, the sun, the mountains around me are "not I", Maya sitting nearby is "not I", the rock that I'm sitting is "not I", the world around me, the earth, planets, and the whole cosmos are "not I" experiences. I'm the subject and everything else is an object to me.

There are two parts to the "not I" experiences, the sentient and the insentient. The sentient, like Maya, can also identify me as "not I" for her. The insentient, like this rock cannot do that since it has no life and hence no ability to perceive. At least I believe so!

Where does the "I" begin? Physically we can say that it begins from the tip of my nose (or stomach, depending on which is protruding more!). However, my body is as much in my experience as any other object. Further, I can perceive my body whereas the body is unable to. Unlike Maya who responds back when I say "hello", the body doesn't! We could go deeper in this to mind, ego, intellect, and consciousness. Psychology stops at mind and some ancient traditions go beyond to consciousness.

The idea of a boundary between oneself and another is not something we are born with. As the youngest of five children, I always thought that what I feel, others must be feeling. What I think, others must be thinking; and what I see others must be seeing too. I got the shock of my life when I realised how far away from reality I was. My Mother reminded me many times not to mess up with my "brother's books" or not sleep in my "sister's bed".

As I was growing up, I realised that there were "things" that belonged to me and there were "things" that belonged to others and I don't possess them. Further, I also realised that others think, feel and do things differently from me and I can't assume that all of us think, feel and act the same at the same moment because we are all different from each other.

This idea of "I" and the "Not I" became more predominant and complex as I grew up. I realised that I'm a boy and girls are different from me, I'm a Hindu and people from other religions are not me, animals and plants are different from me, so too my Mom and Dad.... There was one exception though. My imaginary friends were not different from me, because they were me!

This division between "I" and "not I" was not very easy to internalise. Hence I found myself enjoying the most when I was with my imaginary friends. It was a wonderful world of me and others, the others folded into me and I folded into others.

However, it didn't last long and I was woken up to this cruel reality of "I" and "Not I". These boundaries meant a world of competition, conflicts, aloneness, alienation and slowly the boundaries morphed themselves from "I" and "not I" and became " I versus You" and later "Us versus Them".

The idea of "I" and "Not I" was useful to protect my ego and give rise to a sense of personal identity. This made me strengthen certain aspects of my personality that I thought belonged to the "I" and disown aspects because they belonged to the "Not I". For example I controlled my tears and acted macho when I lost a game because I was told crying belong to the girls. I fought with a boy in school because he made fun of "me".

When I reached my teens, I was fully converted to the world of "I" and "Not I". I became part of the normal. I lived *my* life like everyone else, did *my* graduation and post-graduation, built *my* career, made *my* money, built *my* house, got a life partner to share *my* life with, have *my* child and so on. The world taught me to be sensitive to *others*, put myself in *others* shoes, collaborate with *others* and try and live in harmony with *others* in a community. "Do unto others what you would have them do unto you". I tried to live that maxim sincerely and authentically to a large extent.

My sister sent me a picture of mine taken during her wedding. I was ten or twelve years old then. I looked at that picture and asked myself "Who is this Boy in the picture? Is it the same person that I'm today?" I don't look the same, think or feel the same. My Body, mental formations and perceptions are different. Then it struck me that if that Boy didn't exist, I wouldn't be here today. I'm a continuation of that Boy and if I look deeply, I can see my present self in that ten year old. It is like when someone looks at the clouds, they can see the rain too. Like the rain is waiting to emerge, I was waiting to manifest as this me today when the conditions are sufficient.

The world outside is just a mirror of oneself. Others come in to your life to show you the mirror! It felt like Ayn Rand is speaking to me again ""My philosophy, in essence, is the concept of man as a heroic being, with his own happiness as the moral purpose of his life, with productive achievement as his noblest activity, and reason as his only absolute." See the amount of "his" in her statement. My world, my purpose, my achievements, my reasoning and nothing else matters!

The more I dwelt into western psychology, this concept of "I" and "not I" was reinforced. Fritz Perls, the founder of Gestalt psychology wrote "You are you and I'm I, if we meet, it is great....". Jung indicated that we might carry the generations of humanity in our unconscious, but he still maintained the primacy of one's ego.

A few years ago, I realised that I have been following western concepts when there was home grown stuff that I'm unaware of. This made me look at Advaita Vedanta philosophy (Non-duality). According to this philosophy, the concept of "I" as Ego (called "ahamkara" in Sanskrit) is a thought in our mind (I'm thinking, I'm doing, I'm angry etc.) and is a delusion! This mental construct creates the split between "I and "not I". This split between "I" and "not I" or "subject" and "object" is at the heart of the problem of "Maya" or delusional world. All the suffering in the world is because of this split and the only way out of this is to realise this oneness. The real "I" (called "Atman" in Vedanta to distinguish it from Ahamkara) is consciousness itself and it is one without a second (non-dual).

This fits into what I experienced as a young baby, when I felt oneness with my world. But then, they said, we are we and you are you, we are all different and unique. Now I have come back a full circle. But there is a problem. I have differentiated myself so much that the walls between "I" and the "other" are difficult to break. I know that we are all one at the essence level, I understand it, but in order to live it I have to unlearn all that I have about me and the world. It is my next phase of life journey.

Maya nudges me and asks for my phone. "Your camera is better than mine" She says. The Sun is setting now and the sky is a riot of red, orange, yellow and many colours in between. Nature is displaying a spectacular act to end the day. I stay transfixed on the scene unfolding in front of me and for a brief moment I experience being transported to that scene and merging with it. I feel part of the sunset spectacle and not someone who is watching it. The colours are me, the sky too with those birds flying back to their nests. The lake shines my face and my friend and Maya seem to have merged with me.

I'm very much part of nature's act at the end of the day. I experience the collapse of this wall between "I" and "Not I". I snapped out of it and realised that it was getting dark as the sun is already below the horizon. My friend calls out to me and says "let's go". I check my watch and it must have been 15 minutes from the time I remembered Maya taking my phone to take pictures of the sunset. I thought it was a flash of a second and it turns out to be 15 minutes. Those were magical moments when time didn't exist, space between us didn't and there was an experience of being showered with grace. It just happened. Unfortunately, life beckons again and "I" have to let go of this moment and walk down the hill with them back to the Hotel.

Like we can divide our experiences into two dimensions of "I" and "not I", we can also divide the world around us into what is known and what is unknown. The known is all that is in my awareness and the unknown is outside my awareness. For example, as I'm writing this book, I have my laptop, my chair, and some the contents of my room within my awareness. There are also many things that are not present in my room, but it is within my awareness, like the tree outside my window, the sun shining and so on. Then there are many things that I don't know, though such knowledge is available in the world (we can say, check Google!).

The "not I" world can exist in both my known and unknown dimensions. However, if I don't know something that is "not I", I can learn, and it becomes known. There are various processes of learning available for that. It could be direct perception, inference, knowing from teachers, books or through my own research. While learning the "not I" unknown, we start with affirmation and not negation. For example, if I see fruit in the market that I don't know about and ask the fruit vendor about it, he will not start saying "it is not an orange though it looks like one, it is not an apple, though it tastes like one…." He will just report to me that this is such-and-such fruit. He doesn't correct any erroneous understanding I may have about that fruit and tells me the thing as it is.

This doesn't work when it comes to the unknown "I". The first issue here is that I already have a concept of "I" which is erroneous and needs to be corrected. Hence the Indian ancient traditions start with negation of all that I know as "I" ("neti", "neti" – not this, not this).

What is unknown at one time will become known. But what about that which is wrongly known? I suppose that is me and my first-person experience.

Back in the Hotel, a traditional Indian dinner awaited us. I grew up thinking that food was something one ate to keep hunger at bay. But now I realize how much I have missed. Food is one of the very few things in the world that impacts all our senses. Food is at first a visual delight, followed by a waft of aromas. The texture of the food in one's hand (that's why we eat with our hands in India!) is the next experience we have of food. When we put in a morsel in our mouth, the sound of chewing and crunchiness is an inner auditory experience. My Grandparents used to make a *slurp* sound to indicate how tasty the food is! These days people will give you strange looks if one does that at the dining table. Lastly it is the taste while eating and the aftertaste that lingers long after one has eaten.

My friend has just come back from a Vedanta retreat, and he is telling us all about it. He wants to share a story that his Vedanta teacher told in their class. I was more focused on the food and yet I nodded. Maya is very enthusiastic to listen to it.

The story goes like this. There were ten friends who were going to visit a nearby village. On their path, they had to cross a river. They all swam across the river and reached the other bank. When they reached the other side, one of them had a doubt whether all of them managed to cross the river safely. He started counting 1,2,….9 and said "Oh, the 10th person is missing". Everyone else also counted and came to the same conclusion. All of them searched the river and the shores for the 10th person and they started crying because they thought that the 10th friend has drowned.

A passer-by asked them why they were distraught and crying and they told him "we were 10 of us and we have lost one of our friends. He has drowned in the river". The passer-by quickly counted them and saw that they were actually 10 of them. He told them "Don't worry, the 10th person is here. Let us count". The friends replied that they have already counted and found only 9 of them. The passer-by asked them to count again and one of them volunteered. He started 1,2,….9 and stopped since he was counting everyone else except him. The passer-by took his hand and turned it towards him and said "You are the 10th person".

It is obvious from the story that the friends missed counting themselves and hence thought that they were only 9. Why did that happen? The person who counted focussed on the outside that he missed his or her own presence. All the nine that the person counted are objects that are outside and perceived by the person who is the subject. The 10th person is hidden because he is the subject. It is also important to understand that only when we count the other 9, then we can know the 10th. We need to eliminate all the objects for the subject to become evident.

My friend stopped and I was amazed at the coincidence. I was reflecting the whole day on "I" and "not I" and here is a story that explains it all. I'm that 10th person and I'm part of the other nine. The "I" and "not I" are nothing but me.

My friend seem to read my mind and he said "looks like this story is creating more mental processes in you. So I will leave you alone. Good night". I said "good night" and walked back to our room with Maya, ready to hit the comfort of the bed. I still have the after effects of the previous night's party and the moment I hit the bed, I just blanked out.

"That which truly exists, doesn't come to appearance,
that which appears doesn't truly exist"
Franz Brentano

CHAPTER SEVEN

GOD AND ME

I wake up fresh and feel like I have slept like a log. No dreams, no memory of anything. Sound sleep. It's strange that one loses touch with space, time and objects in deep sleep. All the issues that one grapples in the waking world disappears, including the "I" concept. There is only the awareness of absence.

The image of an Hindu God, Vishnu, sleeping on the bed created by the coils of a giant snake comes to my mind. It is said that the world is a creation of his dream and the world disappears when he wakes up. The world has appeared for me now that I have woken up. Maya is awake and she is in the bathroom brushing her teeth. "Good morning" she says with the toothpaste foaming in her mouth.

I respond with a cursory good morning as my mind is diverted by this image of Vishnu. Oh God! My relationship with God has been tumultuous to say the least. I will tell you more about it after I brush my teeth!

I'm sitting with my morning tea with buscuits and contemplating God. My earliest memories of God were lined with fear. My Mom used to tell me how God will punish me when I did naughty things. Once I took five rupees that was given to me by one of my Uncles and brought ice creams for all my friends in school. I didn't tell my mother about it but the Ice cream vendor did! That evening she made me do 101 namaskars (prostrations) to God as a punishment for my action. The image of God I had in my mind was that of a Police Inspector who was waiting to beat me up when I make a mistake. I hated that God.

My grandpa was a very religious person. He performed pujas every morning and I used to get him flowers, a jug of water and acted as an audience when he chanted mantras. The benefit of doing all that was the sweet prasad (sacred food offered to Gods) he gave me after his puja! This God was a sweet one since he didn't eat the offerings and I could have that every day!

Then came the earth shaking incident for me. Men landed on the Moon in 1969 and they didn't find God there. I believed from that day that science had all the answers to our questions about life and if they don't have, they will eventually find it. Man felt helpless against nature's fury and converted the elements of nature – sun, wind, rain etc. as Gods. So the creation of God came out of fear. Now that science can find solutions to all these problems, we don't need to be afraid of nature and hence the concept of God is not needed anymore. I became an Atheist.

Over the last thirty years I have refused to acknowledge the existence of God and stopped visiting temples, conduct rituals and anything that was expected of a God fearing individual. Richard Dawkins, Sam Harris and Christopher Hitchens became my heroes and I found myself aligning to their rationalist approach to the world, life and the God delusion. In my perspective, God was just an appearance and not presence.

One of the most challenging experiences that tested my belief in religion and god was around the ritual of the sacred thread. I was born into a Brahmin family and the expectation was that as a son, I was expected to wear the sacred thread that cemented my Brahmin identity (similar to baptism for Christians). I resisted that for many years since I didn't believe in that ritual. Once my Mother was unwell and I was taking care of her. She suddenly said this to me "If you don't do the thread ceremony, you won't allowed to light my funeral pyre when I die". This was a shocker and emotional blackmail. According to the Brahmin tradition, the sons light the funeral pyre when their parents die and it was an important duty that one performs. Though I did recoil at the emotional blackmail, I recognised and respected her strong religious beliefs. I did get the thread ceremony conducted but wore it only when I had to attend the rituals after her passing. My love and relationship with her got the better of my atheist beliefs.

Then the next big change happened a few years ago. Maya persuaded me to study the Indian spiritual traditions and after some reluctance I started reading up on Advaita Vedanta, an ancient Indian philosophical tradition started by a person after whom I was named! *Sankaracharya.* I really liked the perspective that he and many others who followed him offered to understand self, world and God. This philosophy can be stated in one line "Tat Tvam Asi" (thou art that) meaning that the self and God are one. Sankara defines God as the knowledge that brings forth the world to consciousness.

Hence God is not a person, a power that punishes or loves based on one's actions but that intelligence which manifests itself as the world of names and forms. Advaita Vedanta goes further and makes a stunning statement that this intelligence is oneself. This means that I actually create the world of names and forms and they exist because they are nothing but me. This also means that I have no one to blame for my miseries, none to fear for my actions or give credit for the good times I have. It is all my creation, my actions and my consequences. The world is that, which I create and manifest in me and I can choose the world that I want it to be.

I found this definition of God very liberating and it changed my relationship with that name and form (God and Deity) because now that name and form is me!

Maya is dressed and ready to leave. I take a quick shower and get dressed myself. My friend is waiting for me at the breakfast table. We have a leisurely breakfast catching up on all the gossip. We step into the car ready to leave. We have less than 100 kilometres drive to reach our home in Mumbai. Maya is at the wheel so I can continue my contemplations or daydreams, as Maya often says!

My mind wanders to the concept of an intelligent watchmaker that was used by William Paley to propound the existence of God. His analogy was couched in a story. He described a person walking through a forest. He accidently finds a watch and wonders about its origin. Did it accidently come there because of its parts falling from the sky; they just appeared completely by chance and accident? Or that it was the product of a designer? According to Paley, someone had organized it, planned it all as an engineer would. In other words, it had a designer. The analogy was that the universe is organized with certain laws, such as the law of gravity. All of space, earth, animals, plants and humans were the result of a designer, God. Just as watches are set in motion by watchmakers, after which they operate according to their pre-established mechanisms, so also was the world begun by the God as the Creator, after which it – and all its parts have operated according to their pre-established natural laws.

Richard Dawkins offered a counter argument to show that the complex process of Darwinian natural selection is unconscious and automatic. If natural selection can be said to play the role of a watchmaker in nature, it is a blind one—working without foresight or purpose.

According to Advaita Vedanta philosophy, there is no creation, the world only manifests in consciousness. The Universe goes through a continuous process of becoming manifest and unmanifest. Then the watchmaker, the watch and the person who finds that watch, it's design, the analogy offered by Paley and the riposte from Dawkins are all manifested in our mind. Hence they are all an appearance.

I have often thought about the philosophical question "If a tree falls in the forest, and there's nobody around to hear, does it make a sound?" There are arguments based on how one interprets 'sound". If sound is seen as a physical phenomenon, then there would have been compressions and rarefactions in the air when the tree fell. Hence there was a sound. But if sound is seen as a human experience of hearing, then when nobody is around there is sense in saying that the falling tree made no sound at all.

Once I had a discussion about god with a friend who teaches philosophy. He brought in a Buddhist philosophical argument which basically says that nothing can be said to exist or not exist, including god. He gave me a metaphor of television and radio waves. He said "we are in this room where there is no TV or Radio. There are radio and TV signals and they might or might not exist in this room since we don't perceive them. The only way to find that out is to bring a TV or radio and plug it in. But we won't be sure that the signals themselves manifested because we got the TV and Radio receivers" When the conditions are present things manifest, or is it that when things manifest, conditions for that manifestation appear?

When I was an Atheist, I used to see this as a physical phenomenon. Then I saw the value in the philosophical argument that any phenomenon needs an observer to be observed as a phenomenon. I would now go by Advaita and say that both the arguments that there was a sound or there was no sound are neither true nor false. It all depends on the level of reality that one looks at it from. I see that this whole argument is worthless since the physical and human experience both happen in the realm of appearance.

So what do I mean to say in all these meanderings? I think that the existence or non-existence of God is no longer an issue for me to dwell into anymore. I'm also completely at ease with a world designed by a watchmaker God or something that is a random human experience. I'm here to live every moment of it.

The car is slowing down to a crawl and I can see bumper to bumper traffic on both sides of the road. "Welcome to Mumbai" said a big road sign. I don't think we need that sign, the traffic crawl is a good indicator that one has reached the big city of Mumbai.

Maya turns to me and says that her legs are cramping and she wants me to take over the driving. She takes the car to the shoulder of the road and we change seats. Now I'm at the wheel and now I need to keep my eye and mind on the road and not wander into the world of appearance and presence. Here a single second of inattention can mean an accident!

"The world is a part of you. But you are apart from the world"
Swami Sarvapriyananda

CHAPTER EIGHT

DEATH AND NO DEATH

The crawling traffic now comes to a complete halt. There seems to be an accident up ahead. I can see an overturned car with fumes coming out of it. The car was on the opposite lane and has jumped the traffic island barrier, came to our lane and burst into flames. A Police vehicle is there and some people are trying to douse the fire. I can't see anyone being taken out of the car, but I can hear the siren of the ambulance coming closer, indicating that some people are either injured or dead in that car.

Maya seems oblivious of all that is happening. She's got her earphones plugged in and is wearing an eye-patch to shut out the sun. So I can't say whether she is sleeping or just lost in her world of music. She is tired too. We have been on the road for a couple of days now, though with stops. I decide not to wake her up.

Some of the drivers of cars have got out and rushed to the accident site. I have an urge to do the same but better sense prevails and I stay put. There are enough people attending there and I don't have any skills in this situation. Further, Maya will panic if she gets up and find me missing. So, the next best thing to do for me is to continue my contemplations!

My first encounter with death in my family was when my aunt died when I was 15 years old. Believe it or not, she died in a car accident too. I remember me looking at the dead body and waiting in anticipation for the body to stir. But alas, nothing like that happened and later her body burned in the funeral pyre.

I asked an older cousin about what happens when people die. He told me about the Hindu theory of transmigration of the soul and how my aunt will be born again and her next birth will depend on her accumulated karmas from this birth. I thought it was a whole mumbo-jumbo without any evidence. Remember, by then I was a staunch atheist! But I was curious and wanted to know more. The weekly magazine called the *Illustrated weekly of India* carried a special issue on "what happens when we die" based on stories of people who had near death experiences. They were fascinating to read and were uncannily the same! It all seemed like a con job where someone got people to say similar things based on experiences of our world here and look as if this is how it will be. It was like how we imagine life in heaven of hell based on experiences of heaven or hell on earth!

The blaring siren of the ambulance brought Maya out of her slumber. She looked at me with a question mark and I told her all that I know and inferred from our situation. She said "I hope this clears soon" and went back to sleep!

After a while the ambulance left and two out of the four lanes were opened for traffic. I start the car as the traffic begins to move slowly. The driver in front was speaking to the traffic cop and I heard him saying "there were two in that car. One is dead and the other is fighting for his life" I thought about them briefly. I don't know who they were and what they did to deserve this. I feel sad for them. Just imagine, all your dreams, desires, plans in life snuffed out in a split second. Maybe it is their karma as my cousin had once told me. I wonder if the watchmaker had this as part of the design or it just happened as a random incident.

The lanes are now clear and I opened the throttle and started to speed up a little.

Thich Nhat Hanh, a Vietnamese Buddhist monk once wrote about the nature of no birth and no death. Not just human beings, but also animals, plants and even minerals share this nature. Everything in nature remains unmanifest when the conditions are not favourable, manifest as they become favourable and again unmanifest as conditions change. To qualify them as non-existing is a wrong perception.

According to Hanh, nothing is ever lost. He gives the example of a piece of paper that existed once as a tree. When we burn that paper, it becomes ash and joins earth and become part of another tree and so the cycle continues. If we believe this, there is no grief or sorrow when someone dear passes away.

I had this question whether we are really born when I met that Baby. If I stretch that, do we really die? The physical body surely dies and gets destroyed ultimately. But what about the mind, intellect, memory and the ego sense of myself. Does that get destroyed too? Like God that we discussed earlier, there is no factual evidence for what happens after the death of the physical body. There are many beliefs though, depending on whether one looks at self as a body that has consciousness or as consciousness that is now in a body. In the first case, when we die, our consciousness (mind, ego etc.) all die with it. In the second case, consciousness continues even after the body dies. Of course, there is a third belief that there is nothing else other than consciousness and the world, including the body is falsity.

If life is just an appearance, so too is death. One might say it is disappearance. But presence is always there, in many manifestations or unmanifest.

The Indian festival of Ganesh, the elephant god, is a great metaphor for this. People make clay idols of this god every year and dissolve it in a waterbody after a few days of worship. When they immerse the deity in the water body, people chant "please come back next year" Ganesh manifested in the name and form of an idol becomes unmanifest when dissolved in the waterbody with a promise to manifest again next year. We too manifest when we are born, we get a name and form and we dissolve back into the earth when we die and become unmanifested, only to come back into manifestation in some other time and space.

We exit the expressway cross the suburbs of Mumbai city and reach the café near our home. This is where it all began in my dream and I want to be here before I end this journey. Maya also gets up from her sleep and says "I was not actually sleeping. But I wanted to avoid seeing the accident and hence kept my eyes closed". I say to her that this is how we as human beings deal with death, we pretend that it doesn't exist even though we know it surrounds us every moment. Strangely, this is one presence that we would rather not have it in appearance! "why don't we just go home. I'm tired" She says. I say that I'm desperate for a coffee and the washroom!

We sit at our usual table, and I order coffee and ginger buscuits, while drooling over the pink and green macaroons by the display desk. Maya is opting for a green leaf herbal tea with nothing to eat. The place appears the same like I saw in my dream and I keep looking at the door waiting for the Mystic to arrive!

"The character of appearance is that it is neither existent, nor non-existent, Nor both existent and non-existent, nor neither"
Nagarjuna in Mulamadhyamakarika.

NON-APPEARANCE

This chapter is unmanifest in my mind since Maya has not made her appearance. Maybe you will give it a name, form and appearance based on how the world, god and you manifest for your Self.

To see a World in a Grain of Sand
And a Heaven in a Wild Flower
Hold Infinity in the palm of your hand
And Eternity in an hour
William Blake

CHAPTER TEN

ALL TOGETHER

I have learned now that just because we experience something, it doesn't mean it is real. Experiences happens at the level of body and mind. Experiences come and go, like the movement of trees and building when are in a moving train. Objects of our knowledge are not independent and created in our mind. The world is a man-made construct and we do construct a world of many with variety of forms, shapes, colours and names. The world would be a dull place if everything had just one colour, shape and form. And everything had only one name. I believe that the many help us to celebrate the diversity and also experience the oneness in the many.

This isn't easy. Our psychology makes it hard. "We have this naive realism that the way we see the world is the way really is," Naive realism is the feeling that our perception of the world reflects the truth and that is the only truth. Let us look at humanity. We come in with incredible diversities in how we look, feel, think, act and love and yet we know that all of us are human. This knowledge is lost when we believe in the reality of our appearances.

Once my father-in-law was sitting beside me in my car as we drove through the streets of Mumbai. We passed by a row of shops with brightly lit neon signs and my father-in-law said " So much of show these days. It looks so unreal"

"Why do you say that?" I asked.

"I think when things are showy, there is something behind it that is ugly. I always suspect that. Otherwise, why hide the real presence?" He continued "Truth doesn't need any window dressing"

I initially dismissed his thoughts as a worldview of an old man. Then it occurred to me that this is something worth exploring further.

The world of commerce is based on what my father-in-law called as "showy". Shops, Malls, advertisements, television, social media etc. sell products and services with lots of gloss and glitter thrown in. One never knows if any of what they claim about their products is real. No one says "I have this product and I think it works. You may want to try and see it for yourself". They say "This will change your life".

The social media, the politicians and the used car salesman have this belief in common – "fake news" will be seen as "real news" when repeated often enough. The whole idea is that if we say something over and over again or if many people say the same thing, it will become truth. It seems ironical that the magic word is for all those who post on social media was "viral" and now the most dreaded word in the world is "virus".

One might say that this is a done thing if you want to be successful with your products, services or even your ideas and opinions. But why do we do that for ourselves? It makes me very jealous when I see posts from some of my friends on Facebook. They seem to live a magical life. They are always happy, they go to some lovely places, meet fantastic people, eat and drink gourmet food and life is always fun, melodious and colourful. Comparatively my life is pretty "normal", more so in these days of the pandemic. I also know somewhere deep down that all these friends who post this fabulous stuff also live a pretty "normal" life with all it's ups and downs, joys and sorrows and all that. The posts that they do are not untrue. But it only speaks about one side of their life. It is like the way we keep the drawing room tidy when we have guests coming for dinner and not bother so much about stuff strewn around in the other rooms.

Why not speak the truth? Why window dress? "why hide the real presence?" like my father-in-law said.

I work as an Organisation Development Consultant and I get invited to diagnose the reality in a client organisation. Most of the time, I need to remove the veils of appearances and projections that are deemed real by people there, especially the leadership. Everyone has their version of the truth and they believe it is the only one. When an outsider like me walks in, it is either to show that we are living happily ever after or that this place stinks, based on your recent experiences in the system. The reality is somewhere in between. It looks like that no one wants to see things as it is or there are so many layers and layers of veiling and projections that we have done, it is no longer certain what is real. People seem to have lost the capacity to distinguish between presence and appearance because it is difficult to believe one's own experiences. Experiences are coloured by time, space and causality and they continue to change every moment and hence it feels like we are watching a movie where one minute there is laughter, another minute there is anger and so on.

Recently I was doing a workshop for a management team and I gave them an exercise to assess how they work as a team. I also gave them some dimensions that they can use for their assessment. The team was divided into four small groups of 4-5 people and they took up this task. After 45 minutes, I asked each of the teams to present their assessments. Then I had a shocker of my life. None of the teams presented anything on team assessment, but plans for how to do their technical projects! I initially thought it was a communication issue and I clarified whether they understood the task. They all seemed to have understood the task and then the question was why they did what they did? After a long discussion, one of the Managers said "You asked us to look at our reality, but we don't want to face it. Hence we looked at our ideal team doing projects". That was a deep reflection. It indicated to me how we tend to fantasize and generate a world of appearance instead of recognizing and acknowledging the presence in the here and now.

I think there is another deeper issue here. Desire is at the heart of it. The energy of desire creates polarities in the mind. Polarities make one go after things that have a positive attraction and avoid those that are negative and repulsive without discernment or knowledge about that one is running after or running away from. Desire veils our mind and projects qualities that doesn't belong to the object of attraction or repulsion. I'm repeating what the Buddha said 2500 years ago as the source of suffering! This is the source of suffering for the team.

Desire is what is capitalised by the marketeers and the social media to keep us hooked to the make believe world. Desire colours one's experiences of our organisations and communities and construct an appearance in our minds. Desire also makes one present oneself to the world not as who we really are, but as the image of our desired self - either the self-image one runs after or one runs away from. This means we are all self-delusional to an extent, but we appear normal because that is the empirical reality of the world. People who are outliers to this normal will be considered as delusional here!

The ancient Indian traditions called this veiling of reality and projecting appearance as *Maya* and the consequent polarisation of attraction and avoidance create *Samsara*. Knowledge of this is considered *Moksha* or *Nirvana*, liberation from the world of appearances. However knowledge will not change the appearance of the world in any manner. We know that the Sun doesn't really rise in the east and set in the west and it appears to do so because of Earth's rotation.

But this knowledge doesn't change the way the Sun appears to us every day.

Appearances and Presence also raise a question: How do we go about our lives knowing that everything – the world, God and my identities are Appearances and I'm the Only Presence? I believe that it will make us more humble, more curious and celebrate our imperfections.

To your Self, aware presence, knows no resistance to any appearance...
Rupert Spira

Epilogue

The journey is over. I'm home in my bed, reading a book. The Journey was a fascinating one, both for the experiences of people, places and things and also explorations into the World, God and Me.

I have gone through my life where I have assumed that my perceptions – sights, sounds, textures, tastes – are an accurate portrayal of the real world. When I stop and think about it, as I have done throughout this journey, I now realise how much I have taken that appearance as real presence. Maybe true presence is beyond my reach and I can only rely on my senses to give me an inkling of what it really could be.

So then, does it matter if the world is "Leela"- a play of appearances? I think it does matter. It is not about believing or not, but it is about having that question always in mind. I think it helps to deal with the world with a sense of "attachment- detachment" make us more curious, less judgemental and more open to direct experience.

It all started with my dream that I had a couple of days ago when we were in Goa. In that dream, Maya and me meet a person who called himself a Mystic. I remember the Mystic's statement towards the end of the dream - "there is only one of you here". I interpreted it as I was the only one present in the dream and the rest were all appearances in my mind.

However, Maya was my close presence throughout this journey. She didn't have to appear to be present, she was always there. In fact I wonder whether I'm the one appearing in her presence. Maybe that's what the Mystic meant. She is the only one here and I'm part of the play in her life space. She is the "Leela", the divine creative play.

In my mind, she is doing some stretches on the yoga mat in another room, unwinding after a long journey.

Through the window, I can see a luminant full moon in the sky, lighting up the whole place. We call it moonlight, though it is a reflected light of the sun. The moon's light doesn't belong to the moon and the real source of that light, the sun, is not seen at all. Moon is the appearance and sun is the presence.

I close my eyes, tuck myself in, ready to sleep and get transported to another world of dreams.